OVER the MOON

THE BROADWAY LULLABY PROJECT
CONCEIVED BY KATE DAWSON
CREATED BY JODI GLUCKSMAN AND BARBARA ARONICA-BUCK
FOREWORD BY JULIE ANDREWS AND EMMA WALTON HAMILTON

ESP
easton studio
press

Jacket and interior design by Barbara Aronica-Buck
Book production and management by David Wilk

Published by Easton Studio Press
P. O. Box 3131
Westport, CT 06880
www.eastonsp.com

ISBN: 978-1-935212-70-6

Printed in Canada

FIRST PRINTING MAY 2012

10 9 8 7 6 5 4 3 2 1

CONTENTS

Preface by Jodi Glucksman — 2

Preface by Kate Dawson — 4

Foreword by Julie Andrews and
  Emma Walton Hamilton — 6

Little Sleepy Eyes — 8

Think of the Moon — 10

A Lullaby for Midnight — 12

Lucky — 14

How Much Love — 16

Jadelyn's Song — 19

Onesie — 20

Every Breath and Thought — 22

It Takes All Kinds — 24

It's Time, Little Man — 26

This Little World — 28

I Love You — 30

Over the Moon — 32

Sweet Child — 34

Yolanda — 36

Winding Down to Sleep (Lullaby With No Words) — 38

The Man Who Invented Ice Cream — 40

Contributors — 42

Special Thanks and Credits — 46

I always thought my grandmother was a wonderful cook. Although mine was the minority opinion, I could not be swayed. My taste buds still relish her red cabbage soup, with which I never failed to stain her tablecloths. Making hand-rolled, paper-thin egg noodles was always a raucous family affair. Most of all, I remember the chocolate chip cookies and the Hershey's Chocolate Syrup cake.

On weekends, Grandma, my brother, and I would often spend the morning at Alexander's Department Store, riding the escalator up and down – just for fun – up and down. Then we'd return to her apartment to bake – sometimes cookies, sometimes cake (and, to this day, no one else can make it, not in the same way). Measuring was interesting; pouring was fun; but the best part was the stirring. I didn't have the patience to do it, of course. I just took a turn. My brother took a turn. Mostly we left to Grandma the strenuous task of smoothing the batter to perfection. Stirring takes a long time, time that we filled with dancing around the kitchen, bowl and spoon in hand, singing, laughing, telling stories, talking about life – not to mention stealing fingerfuls of batter for licking.

Over the years, the cookie batter grew a bit gooier and clumpier. More yellow streaks remained in the cake more frequently. Grandma didn't stir as well. My brother and I could tell that we should really stir more. We did, sort of, but Grandma liked to, and we didn't. So we regaled her with stories of ourselves, and laughed as she shared her own anecdotes and reminiscences.

As years rolled forward, the thrill of Alexander's escalator faded. The cookies required more milk for dunking, to moisten the unblended flour.

What had been a smooth, luscious, rectangular prism of velvety brown chocolate devolved into more of a marble cake – the Hershey's chocolate syrup merely swirled.

In the nine years after her breast cancer diagnosis predicted six months left for her to live, disease, surgery, and treatment sapped Grandma's stirring strength....but never her soaring spirit. Together, we danced until she could dance no more....then we danced for her. We sang until she could sing no more....then we sang to her. We laughed, we told stories, we talked about life until her final breath....and still we talk to her.

My children now do all those things with my mother, a breast cancer survivor. We're grateful for the medical advances that have allowed her a better prognosis than her own mother, whom we all miss to this day, thirty-five years after she baked her last cake.

Looking back, I realize that stirring was all about time together – the most precious gift that friends and family can share. The greatest challenge is to recognize it. It's elusive, ephemeral, and often camouflaged – in the guise of chocolate chip cookies, Hershey's Chocolate Syrup cake, and the escalator at Alexander's Department Store.

Lullabies offer the gift of time in songs of comfort. . . . like singing, laughing, telling stories, talking about life and – yes – dancing around the kitchen with bowl and spoon in hand. Like stealing fingerfuls of batter for licking, let's savor these songs of life.

– Jodi Glucksman

Illustration by Daniel Glucksman

When my husband and I found out I was pregnant with our beautiful son, Zeke, my mind was flooded with thoughts of all the wonderful women I know who also happen to be amazing mothers. I thought of my own mother, my grandmothers, my aunt, and my sister. But one person came to mind over and over again, and that was my beloved cousin Jill.

In 2006, early in motherhood, Jill lost her five-year battle with breast cancer. She was only 45 years old. It was a devastating loss to the entire family and remains a struggle still. Jill was so full of love, joy, hope, kindness, and generosity. She had a profound impact on my life and my soul, and I know that learning from her example has made me a better person and a better mother.

As the weeks passed during my pregnancy, I found myself thinking of Jill more and more. I remembered watching her with her children, and marveling at how naturally she took to motherhood. I found myself wondering what it must have been like for her, towards the end of her battle, when she knew she couldn't beat it, and that she would have to leave her children. With the birth of my son only months away, I decided I had to honor Jill. But how? And then it occurred to me, as if it had been whispered in my ear: lullabies. How about a collection of original lullabies, composed and performed by members of the Broadway community?

I began contacting friends, composers, and performers to enlist their support. I was overwhelmed by the positive response, particularly from my friend Jodi Glucksman. Within days, a wonderful partnership began, and, with Jodi's help, miracles began to happen. The project flourished beyond my wildest dreams, and for that I will be eternally grateful.

What you are holding in your hands is a dream come true. For my part, I am thrilled to dedicate *Over the Moon: The Broadway Lullaby Project* to the memory of my cousin Jill Nicolette Izzi. All the love, generosity, and commitment that went into the making of this collection are the perfect reflection of who Jill was – and still is, in spirit. As a new mother, I love singing to my son, and so I like to think of this collection of lullabies as a way of singing to Jill's children, since she no longer can.

One last thing: Not long ago, I told Jill's mother – my aunt – about the project, and she asked me, "Do you know what gift Jill always brought to baby showers? A CD of lullabies." I didn't know that. Jill must have whispered it in my ear . . . .

– Kate Dawson

Illustration by Victor Mays

Jill Nicolette Izzi with her children Molly and Nicholas

Lullabies have been around since the beginning of time. Every country, every culture, has its own tradition of singing to children as a way of lulling them to sleep.

The French word for lullaby is *berceuse*, which comes from *bercer,* to rock. Whether soothing, humorous or thoughtful, a lullaby is an offering of love, intended to ease, to calm, to reassure.

What parent hasn't experienced the exquisite communion that occurs when cradling a child? Gazing into innocent eyes and seeing the trust reflected there, our natural impulse is to croon . . . to affirm, through warmth of tone and the comfort of gentle words, that all is right with the world.

But lullabies do so much more than provide a sense of safety and induce sleep. Their melodies, the modulated, rhythmic recurrence of their sounds, the words themselves – even before a child is verbal – prepare the way for the development of language, for music appreciation, and for all the related miracles that follow.

As a mother/daughter team who have the good fortune to write together, and who share a background in the performing arts, we strive in our children's books to draw on that background in order to nurture the imagination and celebrate the sense of wonder. We applaud the multi-faceted nature of this project, and the many creative contributions it contains.

This venture is clearly a labor of love. Those who work in the arts are the most compassionate people we know, and every individual who has provided a lyric, a song or an illustration, has done so out of the goodness of his or her heart and in support of a larger cause. The generosity reflected here suggests, as do the lullabies themselves, that in communion, all may yet be right with the world.

– Julie Andrews and Emma Walton Hamilton

Illustration by Barry Moser

Little Sleepy Eyes

Music and Lyrics by Nona Hendryx, Marva Hicks and Charles Randolph-Wright
Vocal by Marva Hicks
Illustration by Sean Qualls

The stars will shine,
Breeze kissing your skin,
As the night begins to fall and sleep
    moves in.
The moon above,
Your cradle will glow,
Lighting your way through the night,
    watching you grow.

    Clouds floating by
    Filling your dreams.
    Little sleepy eyes

Hum along to the song the sandman
    sings,
"Hmmmmm hmmmmm mmmmm."

Sleep, my angel, sleep,
Soon the sun will rise,
And my love will sweep away any
    tears you cried.
Dance with the flowers as they move
    and sway,
Letting gentle melodies carry you away.

Clouds floating by
Filling your dreams.
Little sleepy eyes
Hum along to the song the
    sandman sings.

Clouds floating by
Filling your dreams.
Little sleepy eyes
Hum along to the song the
    sandman sings,
Drift away like lilies on the stream,
"Hmmmmm hmmmm mmmmm."

    Little sleepy eyes,
        Let your dreams take wing.

Think of the Moon

Music and Lyrics by Adam Gwon
Vocal by Brian d'Arcy James
Illustration by R. Gregory Christie

Think of your bed
As if it were a boat,
Still, on an ocean so deep.
Think of your pillow
As helping you float,
Sailing you off to sleep right now.

Think of the stars
Up there twinkling bright,
How they do not make a peep.
Think of the hush
That creeps in every night
As whispering, "Go to sleep right now."

Sleep, sleep
I'm right beside you.
Sleep, sleep
Don't be afraid.
I'll be right here to guide you

So close your eyes . . .
Close your eyes . . .

And think of the moon
As a magical charm
Keeping you safe from above.
Think of the darkness
As me, with my arms,
Hugging you close 'cause I love you.
Whispering, "Go to sleep right now."

A Lullaby for Midnight

Music and Lyrics by Rupert Holmes
Vocal by Vanessa Williams
Illustration by Wendell Minor

Don't go to sleep.
Not yet, my child.
Let's watch the night
While stars run wild.
And very soon
The sun will rise.
We call it "Dawn."
Don't close your eyes.

You've been asleep
Since time began.
Now you're awake,
Take all you can.
Let's be like waves
That sweep the sand.
They never sleep.
Give me your hand . . .

We'll pattern wings from an old magic spell,
Ride Saturn's rings like a gold carousel.

Who needs the dreams that toss and turn?
Life is the sweetest dream, you'll learn.
Don't miss the song this night will sing.
Babe, you and I,
Never say die,
No "rock-a-bye" . . . !

Are you sleeping?
You're sleeping.
Fin'lly sleeping.

Lucky

(from the opera *Séance on a Wet Afternoon*)
Music and Lyrics by Stephen Schwartz
Vocal by Donna Murphy
Illustration by Marc Simont

Lucky the people
Who have you in their lives
To kiss goodnight
To wake with the light
I hope those people realize
They're lucky
And keep you
As a treasure they must prize
Too often we
Cannot appreciate
The things we really love
Until they're through
I hope they know they're lucky
I hope they know they're lucky.

How Much Love

Music and Lyrics by Michael John LaChiusa
Vocal by Audra McDonald
Illustration by Richard Egielski

How much love can a heart hold?
A drop? A cup?
How much love can a heart hold
Before it fills and overflows?
Who knows how much it takes
Before it swells and breaks
With lakes and rivers, seas and oceans,
Cosmic teaspoons of emotions –
How much love can a heart bear?
A dash? A touch?

Too little? Too much?
Some may not think it very smart
That I never learned the measure
Of my own heart.
I don't know how shallow
Or how deep it may be.
How much love can a heart hold?
I'll learn.
I'll test.
I'll see.

Jadelyn's Song

Music and Lyrics by Christopher Jackson
Vocal by Anika Noni Rose
Illustration by Selina Alko

There's a wondrous place made just for you, my love.
Wait for quiet, it will guide you safely there, my love.
Where the sky is wide and bright and filled with every good thing,
Rainbows climb on every side and coquis and fireflies
Welcome the night with a song.

How the moon and stars shine bright with every little good thing.
Clear blue rivers wind through mountains high
And hummingbirds follow to welcome the dawn.
From this wondrous place, I'll wait for you, my love.
Till then sleep peacefully, return to me,
My love.

Onesie

Music by Wayne Barker; Lyrics by BD Wong
Vocal by Michael Cerveris
Illustration by Paul O. Zelinksy

How you arrived, caught us off guard,
Panic and worry weren't hard.
Everything rushed and confused,
None too amusing at all.

Stable but still, what did you feel?
Solemnly we made a deal,
All you could do was your best,
Conquer each test as it came.

I'd heard it sung, babies are miracles, miracles tall.
I had no idea.
This may be so, but you have to know,
To me you were tallest of all.

In a glass box, not much to hear.
Tubing and wires and hair.
Hoping somehow to grow large,
Hardly dischargeable, no.

Forward you sailed, humming along,
Scoring my show with your song.
Each day would bring a report,
Foes of what sort would you face?

You became strong, glass box retired,
Required no more, no strings for this puppet.
Finally dressed, woefully small in the tiniest onesie of all.
Hard to believe, you were too small for the tiniest onesie of all.

Finally dressed, woefully small in the tiniest onesie of all.
Hard to believe, you were too small for the tiniest onesie of all.
Now life with you is full of fun,
But after all is said and done,
You're still my baby in the tiniest onesie of them all.

Every Breath and Thought

Music by Henry Krieger; Lyrics by Bill Russell
Vocal by Anastasia Barzee
Illustration by Tony Walton and Genevieve LeRoy-Walton

Every breath and thought is filled with you.
Every glimpse I caught, the more love grew.
Every lesson taught no longer true,
'Cause every breath and thought is only you.

Everywhere I go I feel you there.
There's no one I know who could compare.
Every time I'm low you're my prayer,

And I try to concentrate on working,
To shake this all-consuming want.
But I spy you as a shadow lurking
In the dreams you've come to haunt.

Every breath and thought holds only you.
All the joy you've brought has made me new.
Every hope I've got is now for two,

'Cause every breath and thought,
Yes, every breath and thought . . .

Every breath and thought is only you. . . .

It Takes All Kinds

Music and Lyrics by Stephen Sondheim
Vocals by Dana Ivey and Walter Charles
Illustration by Neil Waldman

It takes all kinds
To make up a world,
It takes all kinds,
All kinds.

It takes thin kinds,
It takes fat kinds,
It takes round kinds,
It takes flat kinds,
It takes small kinds,
It takes tall kinds,
To make up a world!

It takes strong types,
It takes weak types,
It takes French types,
It takes Greek types,
It takes chic types,
It takes freak types,
To make up a world!

Everybody's a freak –
Yeah! Yeah!
Everybody is like no other –
No!
Everybody's unique –
Yeah! Yeah!
But we're each of us still like
   one another –

Members of the club
From the day we're born,
Members of the club –
Honey, you can leave,
But you can't resign!
No! No!

It takes all sorts
To make up a world,
It takes all kinds –
All kinds!

It takes bimbos,
It takes dumbos,
It takes rambos
And Columbos,
It takes slimbos,
It takes jumbos,
To make up a world!

It takes all types
And species,
It takes hims, hers
And He/Shes,
It takes peasants
And Maharishis –
To make up this world!

It's Time, Little Man

Music by Jenny Giering; Lyrics by Sean Barry
Vocal by Rebecca Luker
Illustration by Cornelius Van Wright and Ying-Hwa Hu

26

It's time, little man
Now the sun's resting too
All the birds in their nests
Are as sleepy as you

It's that time, little man
Come and lie here with me
And I'll sing you a song
Of the things that you'll see

The sun as it rises
The glow of the moon
A world of surprises
All set to a tune

And the earth dressed in green
And the sea painted blue
And the love in this song
That was made just for you

Close your eyes, rest your head
Think of all that you've done
As we lie here in bed
My delicate one

Think of hugs that you gave
And the hugs that you took
And a colorful page
Of your best storybook

For the sun always rises
And up comes the moon
Here there are no surprises
You're safe in your room

And the earth dressed in green
And the sea painted blue
And the love in this song
That was made just for you

Some day you'll be big
Some day you'll be grown
And you'll sing this sweet song
To a son of your own

And he'll rest in your arms
And you'll tell him it's fine
For you'll love him just as I love you
And you're mine

And the earth dressed in green
And the sky painted blue
And the love in this song
That was made just for you

27

This Little World

Music and Lyrics by Michael Friedman
Vocal by Raul Esparza
Illustration by Javaka Steptoe

This little world
Can seem so big
Without anyone to love.

Or this little world
Can make you feel trapped
Inside a ball of glass,
With no God above.

And there's no escape,
It's just the city and you.
It's so big and there's no way out.

'Til someone shakes it around,
And the snow falls down,
Around you, it falls down.

And you see
Another face
Looking back at you
And you realize
It's so little,
It's so little,
This little world.

I Love You

Music and Lyrics by Kristen Anderson-Lopez and Robert Lopez
Vocal by Laura Osnes
Illustration by Gary Zamchick

I love you,
I mean I just adore you,
I wanna do things for you
All my life.

I love you,
I'm not just being sappy,
I wanna make you happy
All my life.

Oh what do other people do,
People who
Don't have you?
They're unfortunate indeed.
Should we tell them?
No, no need.

I love you,
See there, I'm glad I told you,
And now I want to hold you
All my life,
All my life,
All my life.

Oh what do other people do,
People who don't have you?
They're unfortunate indeed.
Should we tell them?
No, no need.

I love you,
See there, I'm glad I told you,
And now I want to hold you
All my life,
All my life,
All my life.

Over the Moon

Music by Zina Goldrich; Lyrics by Marcy Heisler
Vocal by Caesar Samayoa
Illustration by Melissa Sweet

Seeing your smile, I can't help but wonder
What does the rest of the world do for light?
How in the world did you happen to harness the sun?
There in your eyes is a sparkle of questions
How am I going to get all of them right?
Hard to believe that the questions have only begun
All that it takes is the touch of your hand
And I'm higher than any balloon

Tell the cat and the fiddle that hey diddle diddle
It's me who is over the moon
Who could have conjured a thought so fantastic?
Joy can be cradled inside of your arms
Lucky can't cover the half of the way that I feel
Grateful to be here, to join in this journey
Full of surprises and infinite charms
Frightened that dreams are so beautifully achingly real
Thinking of songs that my grandfather sang
Trying hard to remember the tune

Tell the cat and the fiddle that hey diddle diddle
It's me who is over the moon
Learning from your tiny face
How huge a love can be
Tell the cow and dish and spoon
Make some room for me
And though you can't tell me,
   I know what you're thinking
If you could talk, I can guess what you'd say
Who in the heck is this guy with the beat-up guitar?
Watching you sleeping, I can't help but worry
Wanting you happy in every way
Promise I'll do what it takes me to see that you are
And if I can't remember my grandfather's song
Would you settle for Rocky Raccoon?

Tell the cat and the fiddle that hey diddle diddle
Hey diddle, hey diddle, hey diddle diddle
Try not to grow up too soon
Your Daddy is over the moon.

Sweet Child

Music by Lucy Simon; Lyrics by Susan Birkenhead
Vocals by Kate Dawson and Jed Cohen
Illustration by Jon J Muth

Man:
Sweet child, sleep well tonight
Wrapped in the memory of my love.

Woman:
Soon child, I'll hold you tight.
The time will fly, love,
Don't cry my love . . .

Both:
May breezes bring you echoes of a lullaby
To lay your fears to rest.
As if you slept safe and warm
Upon your mother's breast.

Woman:
Sweet child, do not despair,
Cling to the memory of my love.

Man:
Soon child, I will be there,
'Til then I kiss you.

Both:
I miss you,
Sweet child.

Both:
As if you slept safe and warm
Upon your mother's breast.

Sweet child, do not despair.
Cling to the memory of my love.
Soon child, I will be there
'Til then I kiss you.
I miss you
Sweet child.

Yolanda

from an adaptation of *St. Cecilia, or the Power of Music*
by Heinrich von Kleist

Music by Ricky Ian Gordon
Lyrics by Tony Kushner
Vocal by Judy Kuhn
Illustration by Beowulf Boritt

Oh do you remember Yolanda,
The lady who lived by the docks?
The moment she started to wander
Her Ma shoved her into a box.
"Yolanda, my little bear,
I won't let you go anywhere.
Your pale brown hair, your skin so fair,
And boys are flying through the air
To kiss my baby, my little bear.
My fat, little foolish Yolanda,
My fat, little foolish Yolanda."

Oh do you remember Yolanda?
She rubbed soot and ash on her skin,
And when she commenced to meander,
Her Ma took her comfort in gin.
"Yolanda, my gypsy queen,
You have gone to where skies are green.
In Holland now you won't be seen,
You've sailed to visit the Argentine.
My long lost baby, my gypsy queen.
My mariner lady, Yolanda,
My mariner lady, Yolanda."

Winding Down to Sleep (Lullaby With No Words)

Music by Maury Yeston
Vocal by Luke Kolbe Mannikus
Illustration by Peter H. Reynolds

The Man Who Invented Ice Cream

Music by Charles Strouse; Lyrics by Sammy Cahn
Vocals by Tillie, Keegan, Zi Glucksman
Illustration by Seymour Chwast

There's a plaque on a shack
In the front or the back
In the tiniest town called Shoboken,
Or Hoboken,
No jokin.'
And there this man's name and his fame are still spoken
Let me tell you about him.
More than a mother, or sister, or brother,
One person I hold in esteem,
The man who invented ice cream.
Think back a minute,
The thought that went in it,

The dream that he
dared to dream,
The man who
invented ice cream.

He could not
have known
That there'd be
a cone
Or a plate shaped
like a banana.
That people in
Rome,
Or Moscow or
Nome,
Or even Montana
Would shout out
"Hosanna"

So here's to the fella
Who gave us vanilla
Without him,
how sad life would seem
The man who invented ice cream.

The man who invented
    ice cream
The gent who invented
What they call demented,
The man who invented
    ice cream.

41

CONTRIBUTORS

COVER

Revered American artist and political satirist **Jules Feiffer** has created more than 35 books, plays, and screenplays. In 1986 he was awarded the Pulitzer Prize for his editorial cartoons in *The Village Voice*. He wrote the films *Carnal Knowledge* and *Popeye*, and won an Academy Award for his animated short film, *Munro*. His plays *Little Murders* and *The White House Murder Case* each won Obie and Outer Critics Circle Awards. He was elected in 1995 to the American Academy of Arts and Letters and in 2004 was inducted into the Comic Book Hall of Fame. His memoir, *Backing into Forward*, was published to acclaim in 2010 and is now in paperback. Feiffer illustrated the children's classic *The Phantom Tollbooth;* his latest children's book is *No Go Sleep* by his daughter, Kate Feiffer.

ART DIRECTION AND DESIGN

Barbara Aronica-Buck, a lifelong friend of the Glucksmans, is an award-winning book designer with more than three decades of experience. A Smith College graduate, she serves on the boards of organizations that support public education and people with developmental disabilities. She has two children, and three stepchildren, and lives in Stamford CT with her husband Peter Buck. She is honored to have worked so closely on this project with her esteemed colleague David Wilk and all of these generous artists. She herself is a proud and thankful cancer survivor.

PREFACES

Jodi and **Daniel Glucksman** are cofounders of Luckimann LLC, a production company specializing in theatre and film. Together they sponsor the Roundabout Underground. Jodi consults as a dramaturg, and Daniel is an award-winning editor with *60 Minutes*. They are the proud parents of Tillie, Keegan, and Zi, who are featured in this collection. In honor of their mothers and grandmothers, in their battles with breast cancer, the Glucksmans hope *The Broadway Lullaby Project* will make a difference.

Kate Dawson made her Broadway debut as Scrooge's fiancée, Emily, in *A Christmas Carol*. She appeared in *Wonderful Town, Carnival*, and other productions Off-Broadway and regionally. Most recently Kate wrote, performed, and produced her original one-woman show, *The A**hole in My Head*, garnering critical acclaim and four encore runs. Kate's voice-over work can be heard in numerous movies and TV shows, including *Sex in the City, Chicago*, and *The Devil Wears Prada*.

Victor Mays is a graduate of Yale and lives on the Connecticut shoreline. He served 28 years in the U.S. Naval Reserve, retiring as a captain. After many years as an author and illustrator, he began to devote himself to painting maritime historical watercolors of British and American shipping; he is a founding member of the American Society of Marine Artists. His celebrated paintings are in the collections of numerous museums, including the Peabody Museum of Salem and the Mystic Seaport Museum. Victor's contribution to *The Broadway Lullaby Project* is in honor and loving memory of Jill Nicolette Izzi.

FOREWORD

Julie Andrews' legendary career encompasses theatre, film, television, the recording industry and children's publishing. Her Broadway performances include *My Fair Lady, Camelot,* and *Victor/Victoria,* and her many memorable films include *Mary Poppins* (which won her an Oscar), *The Sound of Music, Thoroughly Modern Millie, 10, Victor/Victoria,* and *The Princess Diaries*. Andrews has written children's books for over 40 years, co-authoring more than 20 with her daughter, Emma Walton Hamilton. Her autobiography, *Home, A Memoir of My Early Years* was a *New York Times* bestseller. In 2000, she received the title of Dame Julie Andrews for lifetime achievements in the arts and humanities.

Emma Walton Hamilton has coauthored over 20 children's books with her mother, Julie Andrews, six of which have been on the *New York Times* best-seller list, including *The Very Fairy Princess; Julie Andrews' Collection of Poems, Songs and Lullabies; Dumpy the Dump Truck* and *The Great American Mousical*. She is also the author of *Raising Bookworms: Getting Kids Reading for Pleasure and Empowerment*. Emma teaches children's literature for Stony Brook Southampton's MFA in Creative Writing, and directs their annual Children's Literature Conference as well as the Young American Writers Project, an interdisciplinary writing program for teens on Long Island.

Barry Moser is the prizewinning illustrator and designer of over 350 books for children and adults. He is widely celebrated for his wood engravings for the only 20th-century edition of the entire King James Bible illustrated by a single artist. He is the Printer to the College at Smith College, where he is the Irwin and Pauline Alper Glass Professor of Art. His work can be found in the National Gallery of Art, the Metropolitan Museum of Art, and the Victoria and Albert Museum in London, among scores of other libraries and collections. He lives in western Massachusetts.

LULLABIES *(in order of appearance)*

Little Sleepy Eyes

Actress, vocalist, and songwriter **Nona Hendryx** was a member of the trio LaBelle, and now sings with the group Daughters of Soul. She is also well known for her solo work and collaborations, including her 1987 hit single "Why Should I Cry?" and the song "Rock This House," written and recorded with Keith Richards, which was nominated for a Grammy. She has written music for *Blue*, a Broadway play with music, and scored and contributed 14 new songs to the film *Preaching to the Choir*. Nona is a Teaching Artist at the Tisch Center for the Arts at NYU.

Marva Hicks has toured with Stevie Wonder and Whitney Houston, and was one of Michael Jackson's backup singers on his last world tour. She made her first record while she was still a student at Howard University, and after graduation was cast in her first Broadway show, *Lena Horne: The Lady and Her Music*, subsequently working with Horne for more than two years. In 1999 she was the Helen Hayes Winner for Outstanding Lead Actress in a Musical (*Thunder Knocking on the Door*). Her Off-Broadway credits include *Staggerlee* and *A . . . My Name Is Alice*.

Charles Randolph-Wright has a diversified career in directing, writing, and producing for film, television, and theatre. Theatre credits include productions on Broadway, Off-Broadway, in regional theatre, and on international tours. Charles directed the award-winning film *Preaching to the Choir;* has written screenplays for HBO, Showtime, Disney, and Fox; and has directed and written series and commercials. He has a three-year residency at Arena Stage's American Voices New Play Institute, and was the 2010 recipient of the Paul Robeson Award. He says, "Art is the salve that heals our wounds – I am thrilled to be part of this extraordinary project that heals and helps."

Sean Qualls has illustrated numerous children's books, including *Before John Was a Jazz Giant*, which received the Coretta Scott King Honor award, and *The Poet Slave of Cuba*, a BCCB Blue Ribbon Book. His book *Dizzy* (about Dizzy Gillespie), written by Jonah Winter, won many honors, among them *School Library Journal* Best Book of the Year and *Booklist* Editors' Choice. Sean has also created art for magazines, newspapers, and advertisements.

Think of the Moon

Based in New York, **Adam Gwon** is a graduate of NYU's Tisch School of the Arts; his musicals include *Ordinary Days, The Boy Detective Fails* and *Cloudlands*. His many awards include the Kleban Prize for Most Promising Musical Theatre Talent. Inspired to join the project when he became an uncle for the first time, Adam says, "having it benefit breast cancer research makes it that much sweeter."

Brian d'Arcy James can be seen in the first season of the NBC/Dreamworks Studios TV show *Smash*, the HBO film *Game Change*, and the feature film *Friends with Kids*. He has been seen on Broadway in shows such as *Titanic, Next to Normal* and *Time Stands Still*. A Tony nominee for his lead performance in *Shrek The Musical*, he won the Drama Desk and Outer Critics Circle Awards. His other numerous awards and honors include an Outer Critics Circle Award for Outstanding Actor in the musical *Sweet Smell of Success*.

R. Gregory Christie has illustrated more than 28 children's books, is a three-time recipient of a Coretta Scott King Honor Award and two time recipient of *The New York Times* Best Illustrated Children's Books of the Year Award. An animated version of his book *Yesterday I Had the Blues* was featured on the PBS show *Between the Lions*. He has been commissioned by the MTA's *Arts for Transit* program to create an image for display in subway cars in 2012.

A Lullaby for Midnight

Rupert Holmes has received Tony awards as a composer, playwright, and lyricist. His Broadway shows include *Curtains, The Mystery of Edwin Drood,* and *Say Goodnight Gracie*. He writes that his contribution to this collection is "in remembrance of my sensitive, wise and beautiful daughter Wendy, whom I miss every moment of my life, and to whom I sang lullabies for all of her ten brief years on this earth; in support of this fine project and the many heroic breast cancer survivors alive and cancer-free today; and for my mother, Gwendolen, who also bravely fought breast cancer, and who left this life as she lived it, with courage, wit and grace."

Vanessa Williams has sold more than 20 million albums worldwide and is one of the few artists to score #1 and Top 10 hits on Billboard's Album and Singles charts in the areas of Pop, Dance, R&B, Adult Contemporary, Holiday, Latin, Gospel, and Jazz. For her work in film, on television, on recordings, and onstage, she has earned a star on the Hollywood Walk of Fame and received numerous nominations and awards, including four Emmy nominations, 17 Grammy nominations, a Tony nomination, three SAG award nominations, six NAACP Image Awards, and ultimately a Golden Globe, Grammy and an Academy Award for *Best Original Song* for *"Colors of the Wind,"* from *Pocahontas.* Vanessa is the mother of four, and her charitable endeavors are many and varied.

Wendell Minor has created art for more than 50 children's books. His collaborations with Mary Higgins Clark and astronaut Buzz Aldrin were *New York Times* bestsellers. He has also designed and illustrated more than 2,000 other works, among them covers for *To Kill a Mockingbird* and David McCullough's *John Adams*. In 2013 the Norman Rockwell Museum will host a 25-year retrospective, "Wendell Minor's America." Wendell chose to participate in this project in honor of the family members and friends who have been victims of breast cancer, including his wife Florence's mother.

Lucky

Composer **Stephen Schwartz** studied at Juilliard while in high school and has a BFA in drama from Carnegie Mellon University. His first major credit was the title song for the play *Butterflies Are Free,* also used in the movie version. Since then, Schwartz has won three Academy Awards, four Grammys, a Golden Globe, and several Drama Desk Awards. His work includes the animated films *Pocahontas* and *The Prince of Egypt,* and the hit musicals *Godspell, Pippin* and *Wicked,* which is currently in its ninth year on Broadway. His first opera, *Séance on a Wet Afternoon,* premiered at Opera Santa Barbara in the fall of 2009 and has been produced by the New York City Opera.

Donna Murphy has been seen on Broadway in *Passion, The King and I, Wonderful Town* and *LoveMusik,* among others, earning her two Tony Awards, five Tony nominations, and multiple Drama Desk and Drama League Awards. Her many recent film credits include voicing the role of Mother Gothel in Disney's *Tangled* and appearing in Tony Gilroy's upcoming *The Bourne Legacy.* About *The Broadway Lullaby Project,* Murphy says, "It spoke to me as a mother, as a daughter, as an artist and as someone who wants to join with others to make a difference."

Marc Simont has illustrated nearly one hundred books by authors ranging from Margaret Wise Brown to James Thurber. He has won a Caldecott Medal and two Caldecott Honor Awards. Simont is also a political cartoonist, and author of the impassioned antiwar cartoon book *The Beautiful Planet: Ours to Lose.* In 2008, he received Hunter College's 2008 James Aronson Award for Social Justice Journalism as a "Cartoonist with a Conscience."

How Much Love

Michael John LaChiusa has composed music and lyrics for musical theatre and opera including *Hello Again, Queen of the Mist* and the much-anticipated *Giant.* He was nominated for a Tony for *Marie Christine* (music and libretto) and for the librettos for *The Wild Party* and *Chronicle of a Death Foretold.* In 2006, he was a Drama Desk Award nominee for *See What I Wanna See* (lyrics and music). Michael has written and performed for many cabaret and concert venues, including Joe's Pub and

Lincoln Center. He teaches musical theatre writing at the Tisch School of the Arts at NYU.

A four-time Tony Award-winner, **Audra McDonald** has appeared in many acclaimed Broadway productions garnering additional nominations. She currently stars in *The Gershwins' Porgy and Bess.* The Juilliard-trained soprano's opera credits include productions at the Houston Grand Opera and the L.A. Opera. Audra has appeared in numerous films. As a television actor, she has played Dr. Naomi Bennett on ABC's *Private Practice,* and she has received Emmy nominations for *A Raisin in the Sun* and *Wit.* A two-time Grammy Award-winning concert and recording artist, Audra has released four solo albums. Of her many roles, her favorite is that of mother to Zoe Madeline. Audra's mother is a breast cancer survivor, and the song is dedicated to Lovette George, her best friend, who died at a young age from ovarian cancer.

Illustrator **Richard Egielski,** winner of a 1987 Caldecott Medal for *Hey, Al,* written by Arthur Yorinks, has provided the artwork for more than 40 books for children, eight of which he has also written. In addition to those of Yorinks', he has illustrated books by such classic children's writers as Rosemary Wells and Margaret Wise Brown and the actor Alan Arkin. His own book, *Jazper,* was named Best Illustrated Book by *The New York Times* in 1998.

Jadelyn's Song

Performer/composer/lyricist **Christopher Jackson** won the 2011 Daytime Emmy Award for Outstanding Original Song for the *Sesame Street* song "What I Am." In 2007, he won a Drama Desk Award for Outstanding Ensemble Performance for the musical *In the Heights,* in which he played Benny. He has also performed in the Broadway productions of *The Lion King* and *Memphis.*

Anika Noni Rose was the voice of the lead character Tiana, Disney's first African American princess, in the 2009 animated feature *The Princess and the Frog.* She was named a Disney Legend in 2011. She played the role of Lorrell Robinson in the movie *Dream Girls* and Yasmine in *For Colored Girls.* Her many awards include a Tony for Best Featured Actress in a Musical for her performance in *Caroline, or Change.*

Selina Alko lives in Brooklyn, the inspiration for her first book, *I'm Your Peanut Butter Big Brother.* She illustrated *My Subway Ride* and *My Taxi Ride,* which she calls personal love letters to New York. Her latest book as a writer and illustrator is *Every-Day Dress-Up.* Connected to breast cancer through many friends and family members, she hopes her artwork "can help this project become a smash financial success to help increase breast cancer awareness."

Onesie

Wayne Barker's songs for *Peter and the Starcatcher* won the Drama Desk Award for Outstanding Music in a Play. He composed music for *The Great Gatsby* (which opened the new Guthrie Theatre) and Seattle Rep's *Twelfth Night* and *The Three Musketeers.* In 2000 he began his long association with international star Dame Edna Everage and wrote lyrics for *Dame Edna: Back with a Vengeance* on Broadway, in which he also performed.

BD Wong is probably best known as Dr. George Huang on *Law and Order: Special Victims Unit,* and for his Broadway debut in the starring

role in *M. Butterfly,* for which he won numerous awards, including the Tony Award, Drama Desk Award, and Outer Critics Circle Award. His prolific career includes acclaimed performances on Broadway and off, many movies and numerous TV shows. He is the author of *Following Foo: the Electronic Adventures of the Chestnut Man,* a memoir about his son, who was born with the assistance of a surrogate mother.

Michael Cerveris has earned multiple awards and nominations for his performances in the Broadway productions of *The Who's Tommy, Love-Musik,* and *Sweeney Todd,* among others, winning the Tony Award for *Assassins.* He plays Juan Peron in the current Broadway revival of *Evita,* and has been seen in many productions on Broadway and off. He has appeared on TV and in concert, released a solo album, and performs in the country covers band *Loose Cattle.*

Paul O. Zelinsky's illustrations have won wide acclaim and many awards, including the Caldecott Medal and three Caldecott Honor Awards. His work ranges from his celebrated versions of classic fairy tales to Beverly Cleary's Newbery-winning *Dear Mr. Henshaw* to the much-loved movable book *The Wheels on the Bus.* About joining *The Broadway Lullaby Project* he says, "My wife is a ten-year survivor of this disease. [It is] a terrible epidemic whose cure is important to pursue."

Every Breath and Thought

Henry Krieger is the composer of the acclaimed musical, *Dreamgirls,* which has been seen on Broadway, on film, and on stages around the world. For his work on *Dreamgirls* he received a Tony Award nomination, three Academy Award nominations and a Grammy; the soundtrack for the film version became the number one bestselling album. He also wrote the scores for the Broadway musicals *The Tap-Dance Kid* and *Side Show,* the latter earning him another Tony nomination. His recent projects include a musical adaptation of "The Ugly Duckling," entitled *Lucky Duck,* and the musical *Romantic Poetry,* on which he collaborated with John Patrick Shanley.

Bill Russell received Tony Award nominations for the book and lyrics for *Side Show* and has written three other musicals with Henry Krieger: *Lucky Duck* (New Victory Theatre in NYC, March, 2012), *Up in the Air* and *Kept* (from which "Every Breath and Thought" is taken). Other book and lyric credits include: *Pageant, Elegies for Angels, Punks and Raging Queens* (Theatre Le Ranelagh, Paris, March – June, 2012), *The Last Smoker in America, Unexpected Joy, The Texas Chainsaw Musical* and *Fourtune.* He has directed productions of many of the above in various venues in New York, London and around America.

Acclaimed singer/actress **Anastasia Barzee** has appeared in diverse roles both on Broadway and off, ranging from Lady Mortimer in the Tony Award-winning *Henry IV* to Betty Haynes in the musical *White Christmas,* a role she created. She has been seen on television in *Law and Order, Blue Bloods,* and *Murder She Wrote,* among others. She is participating in *The Broadway Lullaby Project* because "I have lost a number of wonderful women in my life to this horrible disease. I also thankfully have seen a number of women in my life beat it!"

Honored with 16 Tony Award nominations for his Broadway sets and/or costumes, **Tony Walton** won for *Pippin, House of Blue Leaves,* and *Guys and Dolls.* Among his 20 films, he's earned five Academy Award nominations. *All That Jazz* won him the Oscar and *Death of a Salesman* the Emmy. He has directed many acclaimed productions of both classics and new plays and musicals. He has illustrated over 20 books – 13 of them for his daughter, Emma, and her mother, Julie Andrews. In the 1990's he was elected to both the Interior Decorators and Theatre Halls of Fame. Of *The Broadway Lullaby Project* he says, "Having had my own dark adventure with cancer recently, this clearly invaluable project rang extra-specially strong bells with me."

Genevieve LeRoy-Walton is the author of seven books for children and young adults including *Emma's Dilemma, Cold Feet* and *Taxicat and Huey*. She has written four cookbooks with Anna Pump including *The Loaves & Fishes Cookbook*, and two television movies. Her play *Not Waving* premiered Off-Broadway at Primary Stages (Carbonelle Award); *Missing Footage* has been seen at San Diego's Old Globe (directed by her husband Tony Walton) and at the Helen Hayes Theatre in Nyack, NY.

It Takes All Kinds

Stephen Sondheim has won an Academy Award, eight Tony Awards, multiple Grammys, and a Pulitzer Prize. His many achievements include *A Funny Thing Happened on the Way to the Forum, Company, Follies, A Little Night Music, Sweeney Todd* (which was made into a hit 2007 film), *Sunday in the Park with George, Into the Woods,* and *Assassins*. He wrote the lyrics for *West Side Story* and *Gypsy*. For motion pictures, he composed the score for *Stavisky* and songs for *Dick Tracy,* and co-composed the score for *Reds*. In 2008 he was awarded a special Tony Award for Lifetime Achievement in the Theatre, and in 2010 the Stephen Sondheim Theatre opened in Manhattan's Broadway theatre district.

Five-time Tony nominee **Dana Ivey** has appeared in countless Broadway and Off-Broadway productions. In 2008 she was inducted into the Theatre Hall of Fame. Her many acclaimed films include *The Help, Sabrina Two Weeks' Notice, Sleepless in Seattle,* and *The Color Purple*. She says, "I was honored to participate in this project for several reasons: to be in such august company, to sing a new Sondheim song, and to remember my mother, who died of breast cancer."

Walter Charles recently celebrated his 43rd anniversary in professional theatre. Some of the highlights include the original Broadway companies of *Grease, Sweeney Todd, Cats,* and *La Cage aux Folles*, playing the starring role of Albin. He has costarred in the multiple Encores presentations and created the role of Scrooge in Alan Menken's *A Christmas Carol*. Walter says, "I never love performing Steve's music more than when it's for a great cause. And breast cancer research is just such a cause."

Neil Waldman's paintings and prints are included in many collections around the world and in the capital buildings of more than a dozen nations. He has written and illustrated more than 50 children's books and created the covers of seven Newbery Award winners. He has also been honored with a gold medal from the United Nations for a work that became the official poster for the International Year of Peace. He says, "It is a privilege and an honor to join the community of artists in this project, designed to help eradicate a deadly disease."

It's Time Little Man

Singer/songwriter **Jenny Giering** has an AB from Harvard/Radcliffe and an MFA from the Tisch School for the Arts at NYU. She has won the Jonathan Larson Performing Arts Foundation Award, the National Art Song Award, and the Frederick Loewe Award. Giering's well-received debut solo album, *Look for Me*, was released in 2006. Her musical, *Saint-Ex*, written with her husband, lyricist-librettist Sean Barry, opened in 2010 at The Weston Playhouse in Weston, Vermont, and won the theatre's New Musical Award.

Sean Barry is a writer of fiction, poetry and theatre. He wrote the book and lyrics for *Saint-Ex* (music by Jenny Giering), which was selected by the Sundance Institute for the 2008 Theatre Lab at White Oak. It was also awarded the 2010 Weston Playhouse New Musical Award and received a 2011 NEA grant and a NAMT New Musical Development award. Sean's work has appeared in numerous publications, including *Boston Review* and *Mississippi Review*. He is currently at work on a novel. He chose to participate in the project because, as the father of two children, he "is aware of the deep attachment both parents and children make to the lullabies that become a part of their night-time routines."

Three-time Tony nominee **Rebecca Luker** has appeared on Broadway in many acclaimed musicals including *Mary Poppins, Nine* and *Showboat,* garnering Drama Desk and Outer Critics Circle Award nominations. She maintains an active concert and recording career including performances at Lincoln Center and Carnegie Hall, in solo concerts, productions and with symphonies. Rebecca made her cabaret debut at Feinstein's at the Regency, for which she received a 2007 Bistro Award. She is participating because "projects like this help chip away at cancer's devastating effects and give hope to people who are suffering."

Cornelius Van Wright and **Ying-Hwa Hu** are husband and wife, and have illustrated many books both in collaboration and separately. Cornelius studied at the School of Visual Arts in New York City. Ying-Hwa studied at Shih Chien College in Taipei, Taiwan, and at St. Cloud University in Minnesota. The couple lives in New York City with their daughter and son. They comment, "When we first heard of the project, we felt it was a very important and worthy cause. Learning of the breadth and depth of artists, writers, musicians, and organizers involved was icing on the cake."

This Little World

Composer/lyricist **Michael Friedman** wrote the music and lyrics to the acclaimed Broadway musical *Bloody Bloody Andrew Jackson*. With The Civilians, he has written music and lyrics for numerous productions. He is an Artistic Associate at the New York Theater Workshop, and has been a MacDowell fellow, a Princeton Hodder Fellow, and a Meet the Composer Fellow. He received an Obie Award for sustained achievement. About *The Broadway Lullaby Project* he says, "How could I not participate in such a beautiful and simple idea?"

Multiple Tony Award nominee **Raul Esparza** is currently starring on Broadway as Jonas Nightingale in *Leap of Faith*. He won a Theatre World Award for his performance in *The Rocky Horror Show* on Broadway and has been acclaimed for his roles in musicals including *Taboo, Chitty Chitty Bang Bang,* and *Company*, and plays including *The Homecoming* and *Speed-the-Plow*. He chose to participate because "it is an honor to use the small platform my talents have given me to do something that can help make someone's life a little better, because we are all connected somehow."

Javaka Steptoe's *In Daddy's Arms I Am Tall: African-Americans Celebrating Fathers*, earned the Coretta Scott King Illustrator Award and many other honors. He illustrated the acclaimed *Do You Know What I'll Do?* by Charlotte Zolotow, *A Pocketful of Poems* by Nikki Grimes, *Rain Play* by Cynthia Cotton and *Amiri and Odette: A Love Story* by the award-winning author Walter Dean Myers. Javaka illustrates using a jigsaw, paint and collage utilizing everyday objects.

I Love You

Kristen Anderson-Lopez has written songs for *Winnie the Pooh, Finding Nemo,* the original a cappella musical *In Transit,* and many other projects. She is a recipient of the BMI Harrington Award for outstanding creative achievement, and was recently awarded a Dramatists Guild Fellowship for the musical *Storyville*, which she is cowriting. She is married to Robert Lopez, with whom she often collaborates. She joined *The Broadway Lullaby Project* "to aid in the fight against this devastating disease, which takes too many of us mothers from our children far too soon."

Robert Lopez is a native New Yorker and a graduate of Yale. His first two Broadway musicals, *Avenue Q* and *The Book of Mormon*, have been critical and commercial hits and Best Musical Tony Award winners. He has written material for *South Park, The Simpsons,* and *Finding Nemo*. His contribution to *The Broadway Lullaby Project* was written with his wife, Kristen Anderson-Lopez, soon after the birth of their first daughter.

Laura Osnes was last seen on Broadway as Bonnie Parker in *Bonnie and Clyde*. Other Broadway credits include Hope Harcourt in the Tony-winning revival of *Anything Goes* (Drama Desk, Outer Critics Circle and Astaire Award nominations) and Nellie Forbush in *South Pacific* at Lincoln Center. Favorite regional roles include Elizabeth Bennett in *Pride and Prejudice* and the title role in *Peter Pan*. She joined the project in memory of her mother, who died of liver cancer: "She used to sing me to sleep . . . when I was little, and when she was sick this summer I often sang to her."

Gary Zamchick's drawings have appeared in *The New York Times, The Wall Street Journal, Time,* and *Business Week*. He is the illustrator of Henry Beard's best-selling *French for Cats* humor book series and a contributor to Marlo Thomas's *Free to Be a Family*. His wide-ranging work includes exhibits for the Walt Disney Family Museum, AT&T, NYU, and more. Gary is delighted to participate in *The Broadway Lullaby Project* because "My kids are Broadway geeks and wouldn't forgive me if I turned down this opportunity."

Over The Moon

Marcy Heisler and **Zina Goldrich** were co-recipients of the 2009 Fred Ebb Award for Musical Theatre Songwriting. They have earned nominations for Drama Desk, Lucille Lortel and Helen Hayes Awards for their acclaimed collaborations. Goldrich and Heisler have provided original songs for The Disney Channel, Disney Interactive and Feature Animation projects, Disney Theatricals, PBS, and Nickelodeon. They have toured domestically and internationally, released *MARCY AND ZINA: The Album*, as well as their two volumes of Songbooks. Upcoming theatrical projects include *Ever After,* in collaboration with Kathleen Marshall and *The Great American Mousical,* directed by Julie Andrews, premiering at Goodspeed Opera in November 2012. They are involved in *The Broadway Lullaby Project* because cancer "is no match . . . for the love and connection forged between those who deal with it on a personal level, and those whose love is simply too strong to do anything but join in the fight."

Actor/singer **Caesar Samayoa** was most recently seen in *Sister Act* and *The Pee Wee Herman Show On Broadway*. He has played leading roles in film, TV, Off-Broadway and around the country. Caesar has appeared as a soloist at Carnegie Hall, the Kennedy Center and in concert tours. He is honored to be a part of a project that brings awareness and hope for a cure to a disease that has affected his family very personally. "Para mis familiares – nunca te olvidamos!!"

Melissa Sweet's collages and paintings can be found in *The New York Times* and *Martha Stewart Living,* and on greeting cards, book covers, and posters. She has written and illustrated several children's books, including *Tupelo Rides the Rails, Balloons Over Broadway: The True Story of the Puppeteer of the Macy's Parade,* and the Caldecott Honor Book *A River of Words: The Story of William Carlos Williams* by Jen Bryant. She lives with her family in Rockport, Maine. Her contribution to *The Broadway Lullaby Project* is in honor of her friend Cathy, and in memory of her father.

Sweet Child

Lucy Simon won a Grammy award in 1981, with her husband, David Levine, for "In Harmony/A Sesame Street Record" (Best Recording for Children) and another Grammy in 1983 in the same category for "In Harmony 2." In 1991, she was a Tony Award nominee and a Drama Desk Award nominee for the hit musical *The Secret Garden.* She is also the composer of the musical *Zhivago.* Lucy Simon is the older sister of musician Carly Simon, a breast cancer survivor.

Susan Birkenhead made her Broadway debut as a songwriter for the musical *Working,* for which she received her first Tony nomination. Her lyrics for the highly acclaimed *Jelly's Last Jam* brought her a second Tony nomination, a Grammy Award nomination, and a Drama Desk Award. She also won an Outer Critics Circle Award for *What About Luv?* She wrote lyrics for *High Society, Triumph of Love, The Night They Raided Minsky's* and many more.

Jed Cohen and **Kate Dawson** met in an acting class and were married in 2007. Jed made his Broadway debut as Dickon in *The Secret Garden* and appeared in the films *Home Alone* and *Home Alone II.* He is a founder of the crowdfunding website RocketHub. Kate is proud to be one of the Executive Producers of this project. Kate and Jed live in New York City with their son Zeke and their little dog, Sophie.

Jon J Muth's children's books have received numerous awards and critical acclaim. *The New York Times Book Review* called Muth's *The Three Questions* "quietly life-changing." *Zen Shorts* was a *New York Times* bestseller, a Quill Award nominee, and a 2006 Caldecott Honor Award-winner; *Kirkus Reviews* said, "Every word and image comes to make as perfect a picture book as can be." Hyperion published *A Family of Poems,* a collection of poetry that Jon illustrated for Caroline Kennedy, and they are currently preparing a second collection.

Yolanda

Recipient of numerous awards, **Ricky Ian Gordon** composed *Sycamore Trees,* which won the Edgerton Foundation New American Plays Award, and the music for the historically based song cycle *Rappahannock County* with librettist Mark Campbell. Upcoming projects include an opera for the Metropolitan Opera with librettist Lynn Nottage; an operatic monologue, *Night Flight to San Francisco,* for soprano Renee Fleming; and an opera version of *The Garden of the Finzi-Continis* with Michael Korie. Ricky is participating in *The Broadway Lullaby Project* in memory of his sister, who died of a cancer that started as breast cancer: "It is an epidemic that we must stop."

Tony Kushner is the author of many plays and musicals including *Angels in America, Homebody/Kabul* and *Caroline, or Change.* He has written a screenplay, librettos for a musical and opera, as well as many adaptations and books. He is the recipient of a Pulitzer Prize, two Tony Awards, three Obie Awards, an Olivier Award, an Emmy Award, and an Oscar nomination, among other honors. Mr. Kushner was the first recipient of the Steinberg Distinguished Playwright Award.

Judy Kuhn has won an Obie Award and a Laurence Olivier Award and has been nominated for three Tony Awards and three Drama Desk Awards. She appeared on Broadway in the American premieres of *Chess, Les Misérables,* and *Rags*; in *Two Shakespearean Actors* at Lincoln Center; in *Passion* at the Kennedy Center; and in a host of other productions in the U.S. and around the world. She sang the title role in Disney's *Pocahontas* movies and can be heard on numerous cast albums as well as her two solo CDs.

Beowulf Boritt's acclaimed set designs include *The Scottsboro Boys, Sondheim on Sondheim, LoveMusik,* and *Rock of Ages* on Broadway as well as more than 50 shows Off-Broadway, in the New York City Ballet and the Ringling Brothers and Barnum & Bailey Circus. He has received many awards, including a Tony Award nomination, three Drama Desk Award nominations, and an Obie Award for Sustained Excellence in Set Design. He is "delighted to do a little bit to help out such an important cause."

Winding Down To Sleep (Lullaby With No Words)

Internationally acclaimed composer/lyricist **Maury Yeston's** vast body of work ranges from *Nine, Titanic* and *Grand Hotel* to a cello concerto premiered by YoYo Ma to *Goya – A Life in Song* written for Placido Domingo. Yeston's many honors include an Academy Award and two Tony Awards. He has a PhD from Yale, has held the post of Kayden Visiting Artist at Harvard, and has authored a groundbreaking text on the theory of rhythm. He joined *The Broadway Lullaby Project* as a tribute to his mother's extraordinary courage in battling and surviving breast cancer.

Luke Kolbe Mannikus (age 10) holds the national title of "Little Mr. Dance Explosion 2010." He debuted on Broadway as Benji in *Priscilla Queen of the Desert, the Musical.* He's happy to be part of the project because, when he was a baby, his "Pop-Pop" died of cancer, and he wishes he could have known him.

Peter H. Reynolds is a *New York Times* best-selling author and illustrator (*The Dot, Ish, Sky Color, and The North Star*) and cofounder of FableVision, an award-winning educational multimedia company co-located at the Boston Children's Museum. Peter lives just outside Boston in historic Dedham, Massachusetts, where he also founded The Blue Bunny, a children's book and toy shop. Peter immediately jumped at the chance to be a part of *The Broadway Lullaby Project.* "I love supporting stories that matter – stories that move. Move not only the emotional meter, but also move the audience to *action.* In this case, the search for a cure for breast cancer. Truly a story that matters!"

The Man Who Invented Ice Cream

Charles Strouse has written scores for over 30 stage musicals, including 14 for Broadway, among them the long-running hits *Bye Bye Birdie, Applause,* and *Annie.* He has also composed scores for five Hollywood films, two orchestral works and an opera. He has been inducted to the Songwriters Hall of Fame and the Theatre Hall of Fame. He is a three-time Tony Award winner, a two-time Emmy Award winner, and his cast recordings have earned him two Grammy Awards. His song "Those Were the Days" launched over 200 episodes of *All in the Family.* In 2008, the year he turned 80, Strouse published a memoir, *Put on a Happy Face: A Broadway Memoir.*

Over the course of a long and notable career, **Sammy Cahn** (1913 –1993) was nominated for 23 Academy Awards – more than any other song writer – and won four for his lyrics to songs that have since become standards: "Call Me Irresponsible," "High Hopes," "All the Way," and "Three Coins in the Fountain." He was also nominated for five Golden Globes and an Emmy. Cahn wrote hit songs for Frank Sinatra, Dean Martin, and Doris Day, among many others. In 1988, the Sammy Awards, an annual award for movie songs and scores, was started in his honor.

Tillie (age 10), **Keegan** (age 8), and **Zi** (age 8) **Glucksman** are thrilled to make their recording debut with a song by the renowned Charles Strouse and Sammy Cahn. Their many activities include singing, dancing, fencing, sculpting and skiing. They've performed at the Lucky Break Café in Stamford, CT, and the Highline Ballroom in NYC. They dedicate this recording to their Bubbe and Gama, both breast cancer survivors; their Aunt Linda, a breast cancer surgeon; and their Great Grandmother Tillie, who lost her battle with the disease before they could ever meet her.

Seymour Chwast is cofounder of the innovative and highly influential Push Pin Studios. His designs and illustrations have been used in advertising, animated films, and editorial, corporate, and environmental graphics. He is a recipient of the coveted St. Gauden's Medal from The Cooper Union, and was the American Institute of Graphic Arts 1985 Gold Medalist. In 1984, Mr. Chwast was inducted into the Art Director's Hall of Fame. He has designed and illustrated more than 30 children's books and created more than 100 posters, many of which are in the permanent collections of museums worldwide, including the Museum of Modern Art and the Library of Congress.

SPECIAL THANKS TO:

Ron Abel; Charlie Alterman; Gaby Alvarez; Maia Amada; Don Amendolia; Jim Anderson; Julie Andrews; Barbara Aronica-Buck; Anastasia Barzee; Stephanie Bast and David Grillo; Hunter Bell; Jeff Blumenkrantz; Kitty Burns-Florey; Dawnja Burris; David Chase; Doug Cohen; Ezekiel Cohen; Jed Cohen; Kate and Steven Cohen; Coco Cohn; Berta Colon; County Reproductions of Stamford, CT; Roger Cramer; Bobby Cronin; Bonnie and Tod Dawson; Kurt Deutsch; Lindsey Frank; Susan Frankel; Lisa Giobbi; Daniel Glucksman; Josh Gold; Robyn Goodman; Maritza Guzman; Aaron Hagan; Todd Haimes; Deidre Haj; Jay Halfon; Roy Hallee, Jr.; Emma Walton Hamilton; Harmony Color of Van Nuys, CA; Anne Hess; Tim Huang; Regina Joskow; Craig Kaplan; Kitten; Chris Klatell; Stephen Kopel; Mike Krumper; Magalie LaGuerre; Dan Levine; Michele Lord; Man-Can; Rudy Martinez; Victor Mays; Brook Meres; Richard Michelson; Missing Piece Group; Kathleen Clark Moses; John Mulcahy; Christopher Nave; Judy Nicolette; Out of The Blue Films, Inc.; Paul Labrecque Salon; Public Interest Projects, Inc.; R. Michelson Gallery of Northampton, MA; Rabinowitz, Boudin, Standard, Krinsky & Lieberman, P.C.; Charles Randolph-Wright; Barbara Rick; Margaret Rombone; Roundabout Theatre Company, Inc.; Sandy Rustin; Steven Saporta; Steve Schaeffer; Shnug; Matthew Sklar; Laure Sullivan; Ken Sunshine; Joe Symon; Katrin Van Dam and Tony Fross; Valerie Vierengel; Tom Viertel; Neil Waldman; Tony Walton; Natalie Weng; David Wilk; Tom Winkler; Julia Wrona; Maury Yeston and to all of the spectacular composers, lyricists, singers, musicians, designers and illustrators who so generously brought this project to life.

MUSIC AND RECORDING CREDITS:

Little Sleepy Eyes
Music and Lyrics by Nona Hendryx,
    Marva Hicks and Charles Randolph-Wright
Marva Hicks – vocal
Larry Campbell – guitars
Tony Scherr – acoustic bass
Bashiri Johnson – percussion

Think of the Moon
Music and Lyrics by Adam Gwon
Brian d'Arcy James – vocal
Larry Campbell – guitars
James Genus – bass
Bashiri Johnson – percussion

A Lullaby for Midnight
Music and Lyrics by Rupert Holmes
Vanessa Williams – vocal
Taylor Eigsti – piano
Scott Colley – bass
Julian Lage – guitar
Bashiri Johnson – percussion

Lucky
from the opera *Séance on a Wet Afternoon*
Music and Lyrics by Stephen Schwartz
Donna Murphy – vocal
Jody Redhage – cello
Gil Goldstein – piano

How Much Love
Music and Lyrics by Michael John LaChiusa
Audra McDonald – vocal
Brad Mehldau – piano

Jadelyn's Song
Music and Lyrics by Christopher Jackson
Anika Noni Rose – vocal
Larry Campbell – guitars
James Genus – bass
Bashiri Johnson – percussion

Onesie
Music by Wayne Barker; Lyrics by BD Wong
Michael Cerveris – vocal
Gil Goldstein – piano
Julian Lage – guitar
Scott Colley – bass
Bashiri Johnson – percussion

Every Breath and Thought
Music by Henry Krieger; Lyrics by Bill Russell
Anastasia Barzee – vocal
Larry Campbell – guitars
Tony Scherr – acoustic bass
Bashiri Johnson – percussion

It Takes All Kinds
Music and Lyrics by Stephen Sondheim
Dana Ivey and Walter Charles – vocals
Gil Goldstein – piano, Fender Rhodes
Aaron Heick – bass flute

It's Time, Little Man
Music by Jenny Giering; Lyrics by Sean Barry
Rebecca Luker – vocal
Gil Goldstein – piano, accordion

This Little World
Music and Lyrics by Michael Friedman
Raul Esparza – vocal
Gil Goldstein – piano, Fender Rhodes
Julian Lage – guitars

I Love You
Music and Lyrics by Kristen Anderson-Lopez
    and Robert Lopez
Laura Osnes – vocal
Taylor Eigsti – piano
Julian Lage – guitar

Over the Moon
Music by Zina Goldrich; Lyrics by Marcy Heisler
Caesar Samayoa – vocal
Gil Goldstein – accordion
Larry Campbell – guitars
James Genus – bass
Bashiri Johnson – percussion

Sweet Child
Music by Lucy Simon; Lyrics by Susan
    Birkenhead
Kate Dawson and Jed Cohen – vocals
Gil Goldstein – piano, Fender Rhodes
Julian Lage – guitar
Bashiri Johnson - percussion

Yolanda
From an adaptation of *St. Cecilia, or the Power
    of Music* by Heinrich von Kleist
Music by Ricky Ian Gordon; Lyrics by
    Tony Kushner
Judy Kuhn – vocal
Ricky Ian Gordon – piano

**Winding Down to Sleep (Lullaby With No
Words)**
Music by Maury Yeston
Luke Kolbe Mannikus – vocal
Gil Goldstein – piano, Fender Rhodes, accordion
Taylor Eigsti – piano
Larry Campbell – guitar

The Man Who Invented Ice Cream
Music by Charles Strouse; Lyrics by Sammy Cahn
Tillie, Keegan and Zi Glucksman – vocals
Fred Hersch – piano
Julian Lage – guitar
Harish Raghavan – bass

Produced by Matt Pierson
Recorded by Chris Allen at Sear Sound, NYC
Assistant Engineers: Ted Tuthill, Kevin Harper,
    and Owen Mulholland
Mixed by James Farber at Sear Sound, NYC
Mastered by Mark Wilder at Battery Studios,
    NYC
Digital editing by Chris Allen
Production Coordinator: Nicky Schrire